by Steve Brezenoff
illustrated by Phillip Hilliker

Librarian Reviewer
Marci Peschke
Librarian, Dallas Independent School District
MA Education Reading Specialist, Stephen F. Austin State University
Learning Resources Endorsement, Texas Women's University

Reading Consultant
Elizabeth Stedem
Educator/Consultant, Colorado Springs, CO
MA in Elementary Education, University of Denver, CO

STONE ARCH BOOKS
www.stonearchbooks.com

Vortex Books are published by Stone Arch Books
151 Good Counsel Drive, P.O. Box 669
Mankato, Minnesota 56002
www.stonearchbooks.com

Library of Congress Cataloging-in-Publication Data
Brezenoff, Steven.
    I Dare You! / by Steve Brezenoff; illustrated by Phillip Hilliker.
    p. cm. — (Vortex Books)
    ISBN 978-1-4342-0798-2 (library binding)
    ISBN 978-1-4342-0894-1 (pbk.)
    [1. Mystery and detective stories. 2. Clubs—Fiction.] I. Hilliker,
Phillip, ill. II. Title.
PZ7.B7576Iah 2009
[Fic]—dc22   2008007979

Summary: Kayla is dared to sleep over inside a creepy house, but the
next morning, she won't wake up! Her friends must figure out what
happened.

Art Director: Heather Kindseth
Graphic Designer: Kay Fraser

Photo Credits
Stone Arch Books/Kay Fraser, all

1 2 3 4 5 6 13 12 11 10 09 08

TABLE OF CONTENTS

Chapter 1
How I Met Tad and the Two Zombies. 5

Chapter 2
The Pike Street Mansion 13

Chapter 3
The Locked Room Dare 19

Chapter 4
Poison?. 27

Chapter 5
The First Clue. 35

Chapter 6
An Heir. 44

Chapter 7
Shadowing 58

Chapter 8
Debrief 70

Chapter 9
Stop the Presses!. 78

Chapter 10
Great-Uncle Herbert. 85

Chapter 11
Our Fifth Member 98

CHAPTER 1

How I Met Tad and the Two Zombies

Call me Gutter. Everyone else does.

My real name is James Guttierez. But some people think my last name is pronounced "gutters," and also, I'm great at gutting fish. That's how I got my nickname.

I'm good at cleaning fish because my father is a fisherman. See, we live in Tide Cliff, a little town right on the ocean. Only about fifty people live in Tide Cliff, and most of them are pretty good with fish.

I spend a lot of time along the shore. That's how I met Tad a few summers ago, when I was about twelve.

I was walking down by the rocks that stick out into the ocean. I saw this kid standing there at the end of the rocks, where sometimes it's pretty slippery.

I could tell he was a city kid right away from his clothes. City kids always wore clothes that were too expensive for the beach. Tide Cliff kids wore swim trunks and tank tops.

"Hey, city kid!" I called out to him. "Be careful out there!"

He just looked back at me and waved me off. Next thing I knew, he pulled off his baggy polo shirt and jumped right into the ocean.

"Hey!" I cried out. "Hey, kid!"

I thought he was going to drown or something.

But pretty soon, he came up out of the surf right by the beach, where I was standing. And he was holding a gold necklace.

"I was diving for this," he said, holding it up to show it to me.

I had to admit, I was impressed.

Most of the city kids in Tide Cliff are here with their families for the summer. A lot of those kids aren't too happy to be here. At first, they love the ocean waves and the sun and swimming and going fishing, but then they get bored.

Then they just lock themselves inside their parents' cottages, with the air conditioning and video games. I don't make friends with those kids.

But this kid was different.

He was staring up at me, holding that gold necklace, and grinning.

"I dare you to dive for something," he said.

"I doubt there are more necklaces at the end of the rocks," I said with a laugh.

He shrugged. "So dive for a rock or a shell," he said. "Bet you can't!"

I smirked. "Oh yeah?" I replied.

Then I headed out onto the rocks, got to the edge, and dove right in. I can hold my breath a long time, so I didn't rush to come back up. Thought I'd give him a scare.

When I finally got back to the shore with a rusty pocketknife I'd found on the ocean floor, the kid whistled.

"Nice job," he said.

Well, I realized Tad wasn't the usual kind of city kid. I called him Tad, short for "tadpole," because he was kind of puny back then. Now he's taller than I am.

Tad and I decided to form a club. We called ourselves the Tide Cliff Summer Braves, or just Braves for short. We'd dare each other to do things that were a little scary, or a little risky.

That first summer, it was just Tad and me. We spent our time diving for stuff and checking out the old haunted mansions up on the hill.

The mansion on Pike Street is the oldest and creepiest house on the hill. No one's lived in it as long as I've been alive. Tad and I had peeked in the windows and all, but that's about it.

Until one day, during Tad's second summer in Tide Cliff, when we spotted two people inside.

"Zombies!" I whispered.

Tad shook his head slowly. "Don't be silly," he said.

Really, neither of us believed in ghosts or anything like that. I was just playing around and having some fun.

"I have an idea," I said. "Let's scare them!" So I knocked three times on the dirty old window, as loud as I could and very quickly.

The two people inside screamed. Tad and I ducked down.

"Sounds like girls," Tad whispered.

I nodded. "It has to be," I whispered back.

We peeked around at the front door as the two girls came sprinting out of the house, down the porch, and all the way to the street.

Well, Tad and I just cracked up. Then the girls spotted us. They looked at each other and must have felt pretty silly for being scared. But Tad and I decided they must be brave to have been inside the mansion on Pike Street at all.

"We've decided that you two can join our club," Tad announced as the girls walked over to us.

One of them was short and had very dark hair. The other was very tall and had blond, almost white hair, and skin nearly as pale.

"What makes you think we'd want to?" the shorter one said. That was May.

"Well, it's the only club in Tide Cliff, for one thing," I said.

The girls looked at each other and shrugged.

"Okay," said the tall one. She was taller than I was. That was Kayla. "We'll join, then."

So that was the four Braves.

The story I'm going to tell you is how we found a fifth member for our club. And how we almost lost another one.

CHAPTER 2

The Pike
Street Mansion

Curt is another city kid who spends
summers in Tide Cliff. At the end of the
summer before this story, Curt came over to the
Braves one day as the sun was going down.

We were walking on the docks, heading
back to our headquarters with the tacos we'd
bought for dinner.

Suddenly, Curt jogged up to us. "Hey, guys,"
he said, out of breath. "Wait up."

The four of us stopped and looked at each other. We'd seen Curt now and then, but he wasn't someone we wanted to hang out with. He wasn't anything like the Braves.

"Hi, Curt," I said. "What's happening?"

He put on a smile. "I want to join your club," he said. "Can I?"

We were all a little shocked, I think. But finally May spoke up.

"Sure you can, Curt," she said. "But you need to do a dare first."

"A dare?" Curt said.

Tad walked over to Curt and put his arm around his shoulder. "Sure, a dare," Tad said. "We all had to do something brave to be in this club."

"Right," I agreed.

"Okay," Curt said. "What do I have to do?"

The Braves stood there, thinking and looking at each other. What dare could we give him?

"I know the perfect dare," Kayla said. She had a big smile on her face. She leaned down to whisper since she was much taller than any of us. "You have to go inside the Pike Street mansion."

"What?" Curt said.

"Yeah. And you have to bring back the old locket from the bedside table upstairs," Kayla finished.

Curt squinted up at her. "Wait a minute," he said. "How do you know there's an old locket on the bedside table?"

"We've been in there a bunch of times," I said. "This is an easy dare!"

Curt seemed to think about it for a second. "Okay," he said finally. "I'll do it."

As we walked up to the hill and Pike Street, all of the Braves were thinking that we might have a new member after all.

When we got to Pike Street, Curt stepped onto the mansion's porch and pulled open the door. It creaked a lot, and the floor of the porch squeaked.

Suddenly, when the door was open about a foot, a gray cat came darting out with a loud hissy meow.

Curt just about jumped to the moon.

The Braves all cracked up laughing, but Curt got angry.

"You think that's pretty funny, Gutter?" he said. His face was red and everything.

Kayla laughed. "It sure was funny, Curt," she said. "You were scared of a cat! Don't you think that's funny?"

But I guess Curt didn't think it was very funny, because instead of laughing with us, he ran back down the hill.

May shook her head. "I guess he's not a Brave after all," she said.

Tad shrugged. "Guess not."

Curt may not have become a member of the club, but he always seemed to pop up whenever the Braves were doing stuff. Like he did this past summer.

CHAPTER 3

The Locked Room Dare

One day last summer, we were sitting around in the shack behind my house. It's separate from my house, so we get some privacy. It's really close to the docks, too. You can hear the seagulls calling, and the clang of the old boats' bells as they get near land.

The shack is where my dad keeps all his old gear, fishing rods he doesn't use anymore, broken lobster cages — that sort of thing. But there are chairs to sit on, and even a cot that I sleep on sometimes.

The shack had enough room for all four of us to sit around and plan our adventures.

May was the one who started the ball rolling. "I think it's your turn to give the dare, Gutter," she said.

The way we do dares is like that old game Truth or Dare. Except we leave out the "truth" option. One person gives the dare, and the person it's given to has to accept. Or else they're out of the Braves.

I smiled. "All right," I said.

Tad leaned forward. "I think it was Kayla's turn to get a dare," he added.

"This is an easy choice," I said. "The Pike Street mansion up on the hill."

"Ha!" Kayla said. "That's too easy. Come on. You can think of something better than that, can't you?"

Kayla was snacking on these weird dried veggies and mushrooms her mom makes all the time. Kayla says she loves them, but they look gross to me. Kayla doesn't eat meat, though, not even fish. She doesn't eat cheese or fried food or sweets or anything good. So I guess she doesn't have many options.

"I wasn't finished," I said, smirking. "You don't just have to go inside. You have to spend the night inside in one of the bedrooms."

Tad smiled. "Ooh, in the little room with the creepy old photos on the wall and the doll collection. The one on the third floor!" he said.

"Perfect," I said. I got up and reached under my cot. That's where I keep a shoe box of our treasures and things from all the dares we've done.

I pulled off the lid of the shoe box and dug around.

There was the necklace and rusty pocketknife from the day I met Tad. There were tons of cool shells May and Kayla had collected. And there was one long, black skeleton key.

"Here it is," I said, holding up the key. "The Pike Street mansion key."

We'd found the old key the summer before. It was hanging on a nail in the kitchen, but we soon figured out that it unlocked — and locked — every room in the house.

"To be sure you stay in the room all night, we'll lock the door after you," I explained.

May opened her eyes wide. "That's a good dare, Gutter," she whispered.

Kayla popped another handful of her weird dried veggies into her mouth and chewed thoughtfully. "Okay," she said after a minute. "Piece of cake."

"Yes!" I said, and I pumped my fist.

"How about tonight?" Kayla suggested.

"Tonight?" Tad almost shouted.

Kayla shrugged. "Sure, why not? I'll just go grab my sleeping bag from my mom's cottage and head up there," she said.

"That's why you're a Brave," I said.

Pretty soon, the four of us were standing on Pike Street in front of the old mansion. We all looked up at the third-floor window.

"There it is," I said. "The little room in the tower."

Kayla checked her flashlight to make sure it worked. Then we all headed into the house.

Slowly, we walked up two flights of stairs until we reached the small bedroom.

"Here we are!" Kayla said, standing outside the door. "Home sweet home!"

May laughed. "For tonight, anyway," she said.

Kayla giggled and walked into the bedroom. "Lock me in!" she said with a smile.

"Good luck," Tad said. He laughed like an evil guy in an old cartoon or something.

I pulled the door shut and locked it with the skeleton key. "Bye, Kayla," I called through the door.

I barely heard her when she called back through the heavy old door.

Tad, May, and I headed back downstairs and out the front door. We all turned and looked up at the third floor.

From the window, Kayla waved at us. In the dark, with her white hair and pale face, she looked like a ghost. "Good night!" she called.

We all waved back. "Sweet dreams!" May yelled.

"Sleep tight!" Tad called.

"Don't let the zombies bite!" I joked. "We'll see you in the morning!"

None of us knew what an awful morning that would be.

CHAPTER 4

Poison?

The next morning, I woke up to the sound of my friends walking into our shack.

I sleep out there a lot during the summer. The breeze off the water is nice and cool, and we don't have air conditioning in the house.

"Rise and shine, Gutter," Tad said as he pulled the pillow from under my head.

"Yeah, time to check in on Kayla," May added.

I groaned and sat up.

"Okay," I said through a yawn.

I glanced out the open door at the ocean. The orange light of the sunrise was reflecting on the water. It looked like a perfect postcard.

As usual, I'd fallen asleep the night before in my swim trunks and T-shirt. "Let's go, then," I said, getting up and stretching.

The three of us headed out for the walk up to the hill.

* * *

Tad pushed open the door of the mansion on Pike Street. As usual, it creaked really loudly as it swung open.

"Up to the third floor!" May said with a smile. She loved that spooky room more than the rest of us did. We thought the dolls were creepy. She just thought they were cute.

The three of us headed upstairs.

"Kayla?" I said when we reached the landing on the third floor. "You awake?"

Tad led the way down the small hallway to the locked door at the end. "Knock knock," he said, unlocking the door. He pushed it open, and had to duck a little to enter.

Kayla was in her sleeping bag on the floor. It looked like she was still asleep after all.

"Wake up, Kayla!" May said, laughing.

I went over to her and kneeled down to give her shoulder a light shake. "Wake up, Kayla. You passed the dare!" I said.

"She's hard to wake up!" Tad said. He gave her foot a little kick. "Wake up, Kayla! It's morning."

May's eyes opened wide and she covered her mouth. "Guys," she said. "Is Kayla . . . dead?"

I jumped to my feet. "What?" I yelled. "No way! She's just—"

May reached down and grabbed Kayla's wrist.

"She's not dead," she said, sounding relieved. "Her heart's beating."

"But she still won't wake up," I said, shaking Kayla's shoulder some more. "Come on, Kayla!" I whispered.

May was already pulling her cell phone from her bag.

In a few minutes, an ambulance pulled up in front of the mansion.

With the ambulance's sirens wailing and its lights flashing, the paramedics carefully put Kayla into the back of the ambulance.

"I hope this poor girl can wake up," one of the paramedics said.

The other nodded. "Me too," she said. "This type of poisoning is tough to beat, though. Must have been an accident. From the way she looks, I'm pretty sure it's gyromitrin poisoning — it wouldn't be the first time we'd seen it around here, and it's usually an accident."

Poisoning? I thought.

May and Tad and I looked at each other.

Soon the ambulance was zooming off to the hospital.

May called Kayla's mom to let her know what had happened. Then May, Tad, and I sat on the curb in front of the Pike Street mansion.

"I can't believe this!" Tad said. "How could this have been an accident?"

May shrugged. "I don't know. But you heard what the paramedic said."

I shook my head. "I don't buy it," I said. "Kayla's no dummy. She wouldn't accidentally poison herself!"

"But who would want to hurt Kayla?" Tad pointed out. He was right. We couldn't think of anyone.

"Besides," May said, "the door to the room was locked when we left last night, and it was locked when we got there this morning."

"Yeah, that's true. And I had the key in my pocket the whole time!" I said.

Just then, a dirt bike skidded to a stop in front of us. It was Curt. "Hey, Braves," he said.

"Hi, Curt," May said. She glared at him. If looks could kill! May really didn't like Curt.

"What happened?" he asked. "I saw the ambulance pull away."

"Kayla's sick," Tad answered quickly.

"What do you mean she's sick?" Curt asked.

I picked up a pebble from the street and fiddled with it. "She was sick when we got here this morning. She stayed here on a dare . . . from me," I explained.

Curt whistled. "I guess that's it, then, huh?" he said.

May, Tad, and I looked at each other. "What do you mean?" I asked.

Curt rolled his eyes. "Kayla's sick? And it's because of a dumb Braves dare?" he said. "That's the end of the Braves, then!"

With that, he kicked off and rode away.

We didn't like Curt very much, but we had to admit, he had a point. Once our parents heard about Kayla being sick, this might mean the end of the Braves. We had to find out who did this to Kayla, and fast!

CHAPTER 5

The First Clue

"Well, this is the scene of the crime," Tad said when we opened the front door of the Pike Street mansion. We had decided to cover every inch of the giant old house until we found some clues.

"Creepy, isn't it?" May said.

It really was. I was really creeped out. It was even creepier than normal.

We'd been inside the Pike Street mansion more times than I could count.

But now, knowing someone had been there who wasn't one of the Braves, the house was extra creepy. Especially since whoever had been there had hurt Kayla.

"Guys, over here!" Tad called out. He was standing by the back door. It led out to an old porch. We never went in or out that way. The porch looked like it might fall apart any second.

May and I went over to where Tad was standing. "Take a look at the porch," he said.

May and I looked through the door to the porch. "What about it?" May said. "It's gross?"

I laughed. "Sure is," I said.

Tad shook his head. "I mean, yes, it's gross, but look at the garbage out here," he said.

"Apple cores and fish bones," I said. "So?"

"So they're not covered in bugs or rotted or anything," Tad pointed out. "This is fresh garbage."

May shrugged. "So Kayla must have had dinner on the porch last night," she said.

"Maybe the fish made her sick," I added.

Tad shook his head again. "This wasn't Kayla's dinner, guys," he said. "She doesn't eat fish. Plus, she was locked in the room upstairs."

May's eyes opened wide. "Someone else ate dinner here!" she whispered.

Tad nodded slowly.

"The attacker," I added softly.

"I bet it was Curt," May said. She looked angry.

Tad wrinkled his forehead at her. "Curt?" he asked.

"Sure!" May said. "He was even here before, just like in the classic mysteries. You know, the crook always returns to the scene of the crime."

I shook my head. "No way," I told them. "Curt wouldn't do this. Why would he?"

"He hates the Braves, Gutter!" May pointed out. "He even seemed happy that Kayla was sick, because it might mean the Braves will be done for."

Tad scratched his head. "That's true," he said. "But why would he eat dinner on the back porch?"

May thought for a second. "Who knows," she said. "Maybe he was waiting for Kayla to fall asleep and he got hungry."

"But he's scared to death of this house," I pointed out. "Remember? He ran away instead of finishing his dare."

"And don't forget," Tad said, "the bedroom door was locked."

May put her hands on her hips. "Well, I think it was Curt," she said. "And I'll find proof."

Tad looked at me. "Maybe it was Curt," he said. "But I think we should keep looking for clues."

May nodded. "I agree," she said. "Let's split up. We'll cover the whole house faster that way."

Tad ran up to the third floor, May checked the second floor, and I looked around the ground floor.

Pretty quickly, I decided someone other than Kayla — and other than Curt — had been in the house. In the back room, where all the cloth-covered furniture was stored, one big couch had been uncovered.

There were newspapers here and there, and some of them were from less than a week before.

I found May as she came down the steps. "I think someone might be sort of living here," I said.

"Like . . . a homeless person?" May asked.

I nodded. "Maybe, yeah," I said slowly.

Just then, Tad came thundering down the stairs. "Guys!" he shouted.

"What is it?" I called back. "Are you okay?"

Tad took the last three steps in a jump. He stood in front of us and held out a piece of paper.

It was very small, and only had the letter "K" written on it.

"What is this?" I asked, grabbing it.

"K, for Kayla!" Tad said.

"Where did you find it?" I asked.

"Right next to Kayla's sleeping bag, up in the creepy room on the third floor," Tad explained.

May looked deep in thought.

"What do you think it means?" I asked, turning to May.

"I think it means that someone left Kayla a note," she said.

"But there's nothing on it but a K!" I said. "That's not much of a note."

May nodded. "Agreed. So there must have been something else with this slip of paper," she said.

May and I looked at Tad.

"There was nothing else there. I'm sure of it," Tad said.

"Well, then, whatever was there, Kayla must have taken it," I suggested.

"Or eaten it!" May said suddenly.

"Eaten it?" Tad and I said at the same time.

May nodded. "Yup. Don't you see?" she asked, looking back and forth between me and Tad. "This proves it. Someone left her the poison to eat! It was no accident!"

CHAPTER 6

An Heir

We were all pretty shaken up by finding that note.

"This keeps getting creepier," I said, once we got back to the shack at my house. "I can't believe someone left poison for Kayla."

Tad shook his head. "It's pretty scary," he said. "And really creepy."

May frowned. She was tapping on the old barrel we use as a table. "I still think it was Curt," she said.

"He does know that we go there sometimes, and he knows Kayla's name," Tad pointed out. "He could have left that note."

I nodded and added, "True. And a random homeless guy wouldn't have known her name."

May smiled. "There you go!" she said, getting to her feet. "It must have been someone who knows Kayla!"

"I guess so," I said.

"That means us," May went on, "or Curt."

"Or Kayla's parents," Tad added.

May just glared at him.

"What?" Tad said, throwing his arms up. "I'm just saying they know Kayla too."

"Well," I said, standing up, "I'd feel better if we did some research on this mystery person who lives at the mansion."

"The homeless person?" Tad asked. I nodded.

May sat back down and slumped. "Fine. How?" she asked.

"We can check with the shelter on Hollister Place," I suggested.

Tide Cliff is very small, so I figured the director at the homeless shelter might know if someone was sleeping at the Pike Street mansion.

"Good plan," Tad said.

May groaned. "Fine," she agreed. "But after that, I want to go ask Curt some questions."

"After we finish at the shelter, you can ask him whatever you want," Tad replied.

* * *

I'd been to the Tide Cliff homeless shelter on Hollister Place once before.

In fourth grade, my class went there to serve turkey and dressing and stuff like that on the day before Thanksgiving. The shelter isn't a very happy place, but it felt good to make some of the people smile.

I remember thinking that I wouldn't like to think of that place as my home.

When we got down there that afternoon, the director was standing outside, counting people as they came in for an early dinner. I remembered her from my class visit. Her name was Ms. Kelley. She was a tall woman with gray hair that she wore in a ponytail.

"Ms. Kelley?" I said as we all walked up to her.

"Yes?" she replied. She looked closely at us. "Are you kids hungry?" she asked.

I guess she must have thought we were homeless kids.

"No, ma'am," Tad said. "We just wanted to ask you about someone."

May added, "That's right. Um, do you know if any of the people who stay here . . ."

"Or eat here," I added.

"Right," May went on. "Do you know if any of them sometimes stay at the mansion on Pike Street?"

"Do you mean the old Hume place?" the director asked.

I had never heard it called that before. We always just called it the Pike Street mansion. So did everyone else in town, as far as I knew.

"That's the last name of the family that lived in that house for many years," Ms. Kelley explained. "However, it's been empty for years. Why do you think someone is staying at the Hume place?"

"Well," I started, "we found some newspapers."

"And old food!" Tad added.

"Right," I went on. "In the house."

"Wait a second. Inside the house?" Ms. Kelley said, frowning. "What were you kids doing in the house?"

May, Tad, and I jumped back about a foot.

"Nothing, ma'am!" Tad said.

"That is, nothing bad!" May added.

Ms. Kelley squinted at us. "Hmm. You know, I think I heard something about a girl getting poisoned in one of the old mansions on the hill. You kids wouldn't know anything about that, would you?" she asked.

Did she think we had poisoned Kayla?

"That was our friend Kayla," Tad replied.

"We didn't hurt her," I added. "We only want to find out who did."

"Well," Ms. Kelley said sternly, "you'd better stay out of the Hume place from now on. You're only going to find trouble there."

"Yes, ma'am," we all replied.

Ms. Kelley nodded. "That house does have owners, you know," she added. "A family from the city is in town right now, actually. The Pickerings, I think they're called. And they are planning to sell it."

Someone owned the Pike Street mansion? I couldn't believe it. Why would someone own a big old house like that and not take care of it?

"Thank you, Ms. Kelley," I said, grabbing May and Tad by the arm. "We won't bother you anymore. And we'll stay out of the Pike Street — I mean, the Hume place."

With that, I pulled my friends away.

"Did you hear that?" I whispered when we had gotten far enough away. "Someone is in town to sell the Pike Street mansion right now!"

Tad nodded. "I know. Weird."

"Totally weird," May added. "Why would it have to be this week, when Kayla did that dumb dare?"

I shrugged. To be honest, I was feeling pretty guilty already about Kayla's dare. But May saying that made me feel even worse. I needed to come up with a plan quick.

"Well," I said, "if the Pickerings are only in town for a little while, they're probably at the Ocean Side Resort."

The Ocean Side is a resort hotel right on the border of Tide Cliff. People just passing through usually stay at the motel. People with lots of money stay at the Ocean Side.

"Any family who owns a mansion like the one on Pike Street can probably afford to stay wherever they want to," I said. "Let's head down there and ask them some questions."

May crossed her arms. "What about talking to Curt?" she asked.

Tad chuckled. "We will, but we should follow this hot lead first."

"Right," I added. "Before it cools down."

"Fine," May said darkly. "But then I'm dealing with Curt."

May wrinkled her forehead and gritted her teeth. When I looked at her and saw how angry she was, I actually felt worried for Curt!

* * *

It's a pretty long walk to the Ocean Side. The sun was starting to go down over the water when we reached the resort.

A couple was still out on the tennis courts, though.

"Great shot, darling," the woman said. "I think that's the end. You win."

The man smiled and they both went over to the bench for a drink. "Great game, honey," the man said as they sat down. "Good thing that we're happily married. That was a rough one!"

They both laughed at his joke. I thought it was a pretty dumb joke, but it was all we needed to hear.

"That's got to be the couple who owns the Pike Street mansion," I said.

"Let's go talk to them!" May said, and she headed toward the courts. Tad rolled his eyes, and we followed her.

"Excuse me?" May started. "Are you the Pickerings?"

Mr. Pickering put his arm around his wife. "Yes. Can we help you?" he asked.

"Are you friends of Vern's?" Mrs. Pickering asked.

Vern? Who was Vern?

"Um, no ma'am," Tad replied for all of us. "We wanted to ask you about the mansion on Pike Street."

Mr. Pickering laughed. Then he asked, "Are you kids interested in buying it?"

Hilarious. Well, we didn't think that was such a funny joke, so Tad just went on. "Well, did you hear about the girl who was poisoned?" he asked.

"Are you friends of hers?" Mrs. Pickering asked. "It's very sad."

"Yes, it is," May replied. "We're trying to find out what happened."

Mrs. Pickering frowned and looked closely at May.

"Wait a second," Mrs. Pickering said. "I thought it was some kind of accident. Didn't she eat something she shouldn't have?"

"Probably," Mr. Pickering added. "Obviously she's the kind of girl who likes to break the rules and do what she isn't supposed to do. After all, she shouldn't have been in our house. Isn't that right, honey?" He looked at his wife, who nodded.

Ouch. It hurt to hear this man hinting that it was Kayla's fault that she'd been poisoned. But I knew if we started arguing with them or getting upset, we'd never get any answers.

I could tell May was upset by his comment too, so I just kept going before she could react.

"Do you know if anyone is living in the house?" I asked.

"Living there?" Mr. Pickering said. "Of course not."

"It hasn't been lived in for over twenty years, since Grandma Hume passed away," Mrs. Pickering explained.

I thought she seemed nervous when she said it. She seemed to look at the ground.

When I thought about it more, though, I realized that they wouldn't have known anything about someone using their mansion for shelter.

"Thank you very much," May said, backing away. "I hope we didn't bother you."

The three of us started to walk off.

But just when we reached the corner, someone jumped out at us and shouted, "What do you think you're doing?"

CHAPTER 7

Shadowing

"Who are you?" May snapped. "What do you want?"

The guy was short — shorter than May, even — and sort of plump. He had a blond crew cut, and he was wearing Bermuda shorts and a polo shirt. "I'll ask the questions!" he said. "Who are you?"

I rolled my eyes and replied, "I'm Gutter." Then I pointed at my friends and added, "And that's May and Tad. Got any more questions?"

"Yeah, I do," the kid said. "Why are you guys bothering my parents?"

"Your parents?" I asked.

"That's right," he said. "I'm Vern Pickering."

"The son of that couple who owns the mansion on Pike Street?" Tad asked.

Vern nodded. "You just stay away from that house and my parents!" he said. For a little guy, he sure talked loud.

The three of us mumbled that we'd stay away. Then we quickly walked off. I turned around and saw that Vern was still standing there, glaring at us.

* * *

The next morning, we met at the shack pretty early. It was starting to feel weird without Kayla there.

"I'm going to find Curt and follow him," May said. "I know he's hiding something. I can just tell."

"Good plan," I said. "And I'll find that Vern kid and see what he knows."

Tad nodded. "He sure did seem worried about us talking to people," he said.

"Right," I replied. "Besides, I thought his mom seemed to know more than she was saying. When she said it had been twenty years since anyone had lived in the house, it seemed like a lie to me."

"Yeah," Tad said. "I thought so too."

"What are you going to do while we talk to Vern and Curt?" May asked, looking at him.

Tad stood up. "I'm heading to Pike Street to wait for the mystery homeless person to show up," he said, holding up a paper bag. "I've got my snacks ready."

May and I got up too. "Okay then," I said. "We'll meet back here around lunchtime and debrief."

"Huh?" May said. "Debrief?"

"Debrief means we'll tell each other what we found out by shadowing the suspects," Tad explained.

May still had a blank look. "Shadowing?" she asked.

"That means following," I said.

"You guys talk funny," May said, and she turned and left to find Curt.

"Good luck," Tad said, and he turned and left for the Hume place.

Then I headed out to find Vern.

* * *

I was starting to feel hungry.

I'd skipped breakfast, and down by the Ocean Side, there isn't really anywhere to eat. That is, unless you're one of the resort's rich guests. Then there's plenty of food.

I'd been hunting around the resort for an hour or so, trying to find Vern. When I reached the dock, I decided to take a break.

To my surprise, someone was sitting on the end of the dock, with his feet dangling over the water.

It was Vern.

"Hi, Gutter," he said. At his side, on the dock, was a paper sack.

"Hi, Vern," I replied. "What are you doing?"

"Just waiting for you," he said. "Want a donut?" He held up the paper bag. "I grabbed a bunch of them from inside."

I sat down next to him on the edge of the dock.

"Thanks," I said, taking a donut from the bag. "I've been looking for you."

"I know," Vern said, his mouth full of donut. "I saw you sneaking around the pool before. So I figured I'd just sit here and wait for you."

"That was nice of you," I said with a smile.

Vern shrugged. "Whatever," he said. "Anyway, about that girl who was poisoned."

"Kayla," I told him.

"Kayla," Vern repeated. "Was she your friend?"

"One of my best," I said quietly.

I looked down at the water, ten feet or so below us, and thought about Kayla. She was in bed at the hospital, I knew.

"I saw you guys at the house two nights ago," Vern said quietly.

I looked at him and squinted. "What do you mean?" I asked.

Vern hung his head. "I wanted to see the mansion. The Hume place, you know," he said. "It's like a family treasure or something, and my parents have never taken me up there to see it."

"Never?" I asked.

Vern shook his head. "Nope. Not once. So I snuck off when my folks were dancing. You know, after dinner. And when I got close, I saw you guys waving at a tall girl with really light hair — Kayla. She was looking out of the third-floor window."

"Oh," I said.

I felt really guilty about that. How could we have left her there?

Vern glanced at me. "I got sort of . . . I don't know. Angry, I guess," he admitted.

He reached into the bag for another donut. He picked a piece off of it and threw it into the ocean. A seagull swooped in right away and scooped it up.

"I didn't like seeing you guys playing and laughing in my family's house," Vern explained. Then he took a bite of his donut and added, "So I was mad."

I took a bite of my donut, mainly because I didn't know what to say.

"I decided to wait around and teach Kayla a lesson," Vern went on.

A lesson? I thought. *Did Vern poison Kayla?*

"Once I knew you three were gone," he continued, "I snuck inside the house. I was planning to scare her."

He paused and took a bite, then went on. "I heard something out on the back porch, and went to check it out," said Vern. "But when I got there, ready to jump out and yell 'Boo!' or something, I didn't see a tall girl with white hair." Suddenly Vern got quiet.

"What did you see?" I asked nervously.

"I saw a man," Vern finished.

"A man?" I repeated.

He nodded and said, "Yes. A scary-looking old man. He was hunched over, chewing on something . . . maybe a fish. That's all I know. It was gross, and it was dark. And I got scared. So I just turned around and ran away."

I sat and looked at him. I just kept wondering who that man could've been.

"I'm sorry, Gutter," Vern went on. He seemed very sad. "I shouldn't have run off. I should have made sure your friend was safe!"

That's when I realized. Vern thought it was his fault!

"No, Vern," I said. "You were scared. Anyone would have run off."

Vern shook his head slowly.

"Besides," I added, "I'm the one who dared her to stay overnight in that dumb house. It's my fault."

"You dared her?" Vern asked, looking at me. "What do you mean?"

"We're Braves — the Tide Cliff Summer Braves," I explained. "We dare each other to do brave things. It's like our club."

Vern nodded. "I get it," he said. "I'd like to help you find out who that man was."

I thought for a second. Could the man Vern saw have been the homeless man? Was he the one who had poisoned Kayla?

But why would he want to hurt her? And how could he have gotten through the locked bedroom door?

Vern was looking at me, waiting for an answer.

"Of course," I finally replied. "Let's get back to the shack. That's our headquarters."

CHAPTER 8

Debrief

May got pretty mad when she heard Vern had seen someone in the mansion and then run away without warning Kayla.

She was almost screaming at Vern. "You're a coward!" she yelled.

"May, don't yell at him," Tad said. "He feels bad."

"He should feel bad," May said. Then she stomped over to the chair in the corner of the shack and sat down.

I had brought us a bag of tacos for lunch. May grabbed one, took an angry bite, and glared at the floor.

Vern just sat quietly on the cot. And Tad and I looked at each other.

After a few moments of silence, I decided to break the ice. I had to say something. It was getting way too tense in there.

"So, anyway, you all know what I found out now," I said. "May, what did you find out about Curt?"

May chewed another bite of her taco for a second. With her mouth full, she said, "Nothing much. Curt is a total bore. He was sitting in his parents' cottage all morning, with his thumbs going crazy on his video game controller."

Tad laughed. "Sounds like you got the easy job," he joked.

May shrugged and went on, "After a little while I got bored. So I knocked. Curt's mom answered, and so I asked her if she knew where Curt had been two nights ago."

"Very direct!" I said with a chuckle.

"I know," May said, smiling. "But anyway, Curt was with her and his dad at dinner, and then the three of them went right back to the cottage. He didn't leave again until the morning, when he went for a bike ride."

"And that's when we saw him," I added.

May nodded. She said, "So since that was a total dead end, I decided to head to the resort to see what the Pickerings were up to. All they did was play tennis and eat oysters and cheese for an early lunch. All in all, I had a boring morning!"

Vern smiled. "That's my parents. Boring," he said, rolling his eyes.

May smiled back at him.

I breathed a sigh of relief. She wasn't going to kill him after all.

"What about you, Tad?" I asked.

"Well," Tad started, "I didn't have long to wait when I got to the Hume place. The mystery guy — probably the same guy Vern saw — was walking out of the back door when I got there."

"Whoa!" I said. "Was he scary?"

Tad shrugged. "Not really. Just kind of sad," he said.

Vern looked at the floor.

Tad noticed, and added, "I mean, he probably would have seemed scary at night, hunched over, inside the creepy Hume place."

Vern looked up and nodded. "He definitely was creepy," he said.

Tad went on, "I followed him for a pretty long time. He walked all over town. Finally he reached a campsite on the beach by the Ocean Side. It looked like that was his main spot to hang out."

Tad took a bite out of his taco and chewed for a little while.

"Come on, Tad!" I said. "Hurry it up. You're getting to the good part!"

Tad laughed. Then he said, "Well, then I watched him for a while. Most of the time he was mumbling to himself."

"What was he saying?" May asked.

Tad shrugged. "It was hard to tell, but maybe 'little girl'? I also watched him do some fishing and sit around for a while and clean some mushrooms."

"Mushrooms?" I said. "What for?"

"Who knows," Tad said. "To make a sauce for his fish? I don't like mushrooms. If Kayla were there, she probably would've known what they were."

We all got quiet.

We were doing everything we could to find out who had poisoned Kayla. But it was really hard to hear her name out loud without feeling sad.

"Anyway," Tad said after a second, "pretty soon he got up to walk into the woods. That's where I was watching him from. So I got out of there before he saw me."

I scratched my head. "Tennis players, video gamers, mushroom eaters . . . and you, Vern," I said. "And I still have no idea what it all means!"

May nodded. "I know," she said. "No closer to figuring out who poisoned Kayla."

"Well," Tad said, walking over to Vern, "we do have someone who knows about that house. And he's standing right here."

May and I stood up and joined Tad. We stood over Vern and looked down at him.

"So, Vern," I said. "What else do you know?"

CHAPTER 9

Stop the Presses!

Vern swallowed hard. I guess he wasn't ready for our questions. "Um, guys?" he said, wriggling back on the cot, trying to get back from us.

"Just tell us whatever you know about the Hume place, Vern," May said. "Like, how did your family get it? Your name is Pickering, not Hume."

Vern shook his head. "It's not anything weird, I swear! My mom's maiden name is Hume. Abigail Hume."

"Go on," Tad said.

"Well," Vern continued, "she inherited the house when my great-uncle, Herbert Hume, disappeared eight years ago."

"What happened to him?" I asked.

Vern shrugged. "No one knows. But he was Great-Grandma Hume's son, my mom's uncle. And when he disappeared, my mom took over owning the house and paying the taxes and all that stuff."

"Wait a minute," I said. "Your mom said no one had lived in the house since Grandma Hume died, twenty years ago."

Vern glanced back and forth. He looked nervous.

May leaned in at him. "Yeah, so what about your uncle?" she asked. "That's twelve years from when Grandma Hume died to when Uncle Herbert went missing!"

"I don't know," Vern said. "Mom never talks about Uncle Herbert."

Tad, May, and I exchanged a glance. There was something important missing. We could tell. But it was clear that Vern wasn't going to tell us anything. I wasn't even sure he knew any more of the story.

"So, why are you guys selling it now?" Tad asked.

"My dad said he was tired of paying taxes on a house we never used," Vern said.

I stood thinking everything over. An old guy cleaning mushrooms. A mystery uncle. A rich couple from the city. Somehow, it all had to fit together. But how did it add up?

Just then, my dad knocked on the shack door. Even though it was his shack, he always knocked when the Braves were meeting.

"Come on in, Dad," I called out.

He stuck his head in. "Hi, kids," he said. "James, I thought you might want to see the paper this morning. There's a story about your friend in here." He threw the paper into the shack.

"I'll see you later for supper, right?" Dad asked me.

I nodded and said, "You got it, Dad." Then he left.

Tad grabbed the paper. A big photo of Kayla was right on the front page. And next to it was a photo of Mrs. Pickering.

"Hey, Vern, it's your mom," Tad said.

"Yeah, they called last night to interview her for that story," Vern explained. "But who's that?"

He pointed to a third photo. It was an old man, and the photo looked about ten years old.

Tad squinted at the caption and read out loud, "Herbert Hume, former owner of the house on Pike Street, before his disappearance eight years ago."

"My great-uncle Herbert?" Vern said. He grabbed the paper and stared at the picture. "Whoa."

"You recognize him?" I asked.

Vern shook his head and said, "I've never met my great-uncle. Never seen him before in my life."

Tad grabbed the paper back and looked at the photo of Herbert Hume. "Well, I recognize him," he said, smiling.

"You recognize him?" May and I said together.

"How is that possible?" Vern asked, getting to his feet. "You'd never even heard of him until today!"

Tad only smiled and shook his head. "I'll explain in a second, but first I need to check something." He turned to me. "You have a laptop, right, Gutter?" he asked.

"Yes," I replied. "Want me to get it?"

Tad nodded. "Yup," he said. "I think I figured this whole thing out, but I need to look up 'gyromitrin.'"

CHAPTER 10

Great-Uncle Herbert

An hour later, we were walking in the woods north of Ocean Side Resort.

"Not far now," Tad said. "Just a little ways past this next clearing."

"I'm a little scared," Vern said.

May poked his shoulder. "You would be," she said.

Vern looked hurt, and May didn't apologize. I knew May was upset about Kayla, but I didn't think it was fair to blame Vern.

Suddenly Tad stopped. "Quiet," he whispered.

I could hear some waves breaking lightly. We had obviously reached the beach, but we still couldn't quite see the shore because of the thick plant growth.

"It's right over there," Tad whispered to us. He stepped to the edge of the woods and pushed aside some branches.

Vern, May, and I squinted through the opening. Through it, I was able to spot a tent on the beach, along with a campfire and some camping gear. A man was standing there.

"Let's get a little closer," Vern said.

"He might see us!" May snapped.

Vern glared at her. "I'm no coward," he said, crossing his arms. "Come on. Let's move closer."

We carefully crept closer, around the back of the tent. Suddenly Tad stepped on a dry twig. It broke with a loud crack. We all froze, waiting for the man to turn and spot us. But he didn't even move.

"He must be kind of out of it," May said.

Vern nodded and said, "He's mumbling to himself. Listen."

I tried to hear. Like Tad had said, it sounded like "little girl." I also thought he might have said "Abby."

"Did you hear that?" I asked the others.

May nodded. "He said Abby. But who's Abby?" she asked.

"Time to find out," Vern said. With that, he stepped out onto the beach and walked right up to the homeless man.

"Wait, Vern!" May whispered.

Vern didn't stop. Instead, he walked right up to the man.

He was pretty brave after all!

"Uncle Herbert?" Vern said as the man looked up.

For a second, it looked like the man smiled, but then he just grimaced and started mumbling some more.

"Uncle Herbert," Vern went on, "did you poison that little girl in the house?"

The man shook his head and turned away. "I'm not your uncle, little boy," he said. "I'm Abby's uncle."

There was that name again.

"Little Abby," the man went on. "I haven't seen her in years. My sweet niece Abby."

"Uncle Herbert, are you talking about Abby Hume?" Vern asked.

"Stop calling me uncle, boy!" the man shouted. "Of course I mean Abby Hume. My sweet little niece."

Abby is short for Abigail, I realized suddenly. Abigail Hume, Vern's mother! It was Uncle Herbert after all.

"She used to stay with me and Mother at the house," Herbert continued.

He was crying now, and it seemed like his thoughts were far away.

He gazed out at the ocean. "We had the room at the top of the stairs all set up for her, with little dollies and family photos. She loved those photos and those dolls."

"Abigail Hume is my mother, Uncle Herbert," Vern explained.

It didn't seem like Herbert heard him. He just kept talking.

"She used to come over so often," he went on. "But then she stopped coming. I missed her so much."

Herbert sat on the sand and held his head. He cried a little, and kept mumbling his niece's name.

After a moment, he looked up at Vern, as though seeing him for the first time. "I missed her so much . . . until the other night."

"What happened the other night?" May said gently as she stepped out into the clearing. Tad and I joined her.

Herbert didn't even move as we all walked over to him. I couldn't even be sure that he knew anyone was there at all besides him and Vern.

"Abby was there again," he said, still crying. "In her old room, at the top of the stairs."

Tad elbowed me. "Don't you get it?" he said. "He saw Kayla, and he thought it was his niece, like, thirty years ago."

I nodded.

It was all becoming clear. But I still had one important question. Why had he poisoned her?

"Were you mad at little Abby, for never visiting anymore?" Vern asked.

Herbert looked shocked. "Mad at her?" he said. "At little Abby? Of course not!"

"But . . . why did you . . ." May started.

"I would never be mad at Abby," Herbert said. "No, no. I brought her a snack, though. She always had the strangest taste for food."

Herbert laughed lightly and went on. "Even when she was a tiny baby, she loved to snack on dried mushrooms."

Vern's mouth dropped open. "It's true! She eats dried veggies and stuff all the time. She says they're the healthiest food around!"

"Just like Kayla!" Tad whispered to me. I nodded.

"So I gathered some mushrooms from the woods and cleaned them for her and dried them by the fire," Herbert went on.

He looked out at the ocean again.

"She had locked the door, I guess," he said with a soft laugh. "Abby always liked playing with the old keys in Mother's house."

Herbert looked down at his ragged shirt. He opened the top button and pulled out a leather necklace.

A long black skeleton key dangled from it.

"I hardly use this key anymore," he said. "No need to lock the doors these days."

"There's another copy of the key?" I asked.

Herbert nodded, his face blank. "One for Mother, one for Herbert, and one for little Abby to play with," he said.

Vern gently asked, "So you brought her a snack?"

Herbert nodded again. "But I didn't want to wake her up. She looked so sweet sleeping there. So I left her a pile of mushrooms and a little note."

"Wait a second," Tad whispered to me. "That note had a 'K' on it."

"I know," I whispered back. "I don't get it."

"A little note," Herbert went on. "With an 'A' for Abby."

"Look at this," May whispered.

She pulled the note with the 'K' out of her pocket.

But when she turned it, it did look like an 'A'. "He didn't write 'K,'" May added. "He wrote 'A.' We just thought it said 'K.'"

Herbert nodded and said, "Then I locked the door up tight again when I left."

And with that, he went back to his campfire and turned a piece of fish he had cooking.

"Kayla must have thought one of us had come in and left her a snack," May said. "She thought it was a 'K' too."

"Right," I added. "I mean, who else knows she likes dried mushrooms?"

Vern made a face. "Gross," he said. "But still, why did Herbert give her poisonous mushrooms?"

Tad smiled. "I know this one," he said. "And it's why the paramedics thought it had been an accident. Morels!"

"Morels?" I asked. "Huh?"

"They're a kind of mushroom," Tad went on. "They're a mushroom for eating, in fact. But there's a wild mushroom that looks just like them, and it's very poisonous."

"Gyro — whatsit?" May said.

"Gyromitrin," Tad said. "Right. It's the poison the fake morels have if you don't boil them for, like, hours. According to the website I found, anyway. And that's what the paramedics said was wrong with Kayla."

"So Herbert didn't mean to give her poison," Vern said with a sigh. "He just thought he was giving her morels for a snack."

"Then it was an accident after all," May said quietly.

I shrugged. "Sort of," I said.

"Can I use your phone, May, please?" Vern asked.

May pulled out her cell phone and handed it to him.

"Calling the cops?" Tad asked.

Vern shook his head. "Ocean Side Resort," he said. "I thought I'd let Mom know her favorite uncle — and the real owner of the Pike Street mansion — is out here."

CHAPTER 11

Our Fifth Member

Kayla finally woke up the next morning. The doctors said she'd be fine, and there were no lasting problems.

"You got so lucky," Tad said when we all met up that night. "Gyromitrin can kill you, or at least cause serious problems."

"I know," Kayla said with a smile. "I'm also lucky I have friends like the Braves."

All of us, plus Vern, were sitting on a railing on the beach, near the shack.

I could smell fish cooking at the taco stand, and I could feel the cool salty breeze coming off the ocean. And it was great to see Kayla's smiling face again.

"We're all really glad you're okay, Kayla," May said.

"We sure are," I added.

Kayla smiled at us. "I'm glad to be okay!" she said with a laugh.

"So, Vern," I asked, "have your folks sold that house yet?"

"Didn't you hear?" Vern replied. "We're not going to sell it."

"Why not?" Tad asked.

"Well," said Vern, "since Uncle Herbert has been found, Mom decided it wouldn't be right to sell the house out from under him. So, Dad agreed to pay to have it fixed up safe again."

"Herbert's going to live there alone?" Tad asked.

Vern shook his head. "Not on his own," he said. "He's not . . . healthy enough for that."

We knew he meant his uncle was a little crazy, but no one said anything about it.

"Mom's going to hire a nurse to take care of Uncle Herbert and live in the house with him," Vern explained. "I think Mom and Dad feel bad for lying about him for so long."

"Lying?" I asked. "You mean because they said that no one had lived in the house after Grandma Hume died?"

Vern nodded. "Mom was embarrassed that her uncle had, you know, gone mad. So she never admitted that he even existed."

"How did the newspaper find out?" May asked. "Your mom wouldn't have told them during that interview, would she?"

"She must have known it would come out, what with them selling the house and everything," Tad said, leaning back.

Vern nodded. "Right. They check a house's history when it's being sold," he explained. "I guess Mom decided to come clean."

We were quiet for a minute. Maybe we were all thinking what a big deal that dare I'd given Kayla had turned out to be.

Then Vern smiled and said, "The best news is that my family will keep coming here for summers. We'll stay in the house with Great-Uncle Herbert."

"So you're going to be a Tide Cliffer now?" I asked, smiling.

Vern nodded. "Over the summers I will be!" he replied.

Tad gave Vern a high five and said, "Nice."

Vern laughed. "It's a cool town," he said. "Definitely not boring!"

"Well," I said, "we like to keep things interesting around here."

Kayla frowned. "Hopefully things won't be this interesting for a while!" she said.

Tad laughed and patted her on the back. "No dares for you for a while," he said.

"You sure proved yourself, Vern," May said. Then she added shyly, "I'm sorry I called you a coward."

Vern smiled. "That's okay," he said kindly.

"I think he could probably skip initiation," Tad said. He looked at me, Kayla, and May.

I laughed. "For sure," I replied.

"What do you mean?" Vern asked.

Kayla hopped down from the railing and smiled at Vern.

"Initiation. The test you have to pass. To join the Tide Cliff Summer Braves!" Kayla said. "You've already shown how brave you are."

"Right," I added. "You're a member now."

"If you want to join," May added.

Vern beamed. "You bet I do," he said.

So that's how we met the fifth Brave.

That was a great summer, but as usual, it ended way too quickly. Soon it was just me in Tide Cliff, going to school, cleaning fish with my dad.

In Tide Cliff, another summer is always around the corner. I knew Tad, May, Kayla, and Vern would be back soon. Soon we'd have more great adventures.

But I can't tell you about those right now. Some other time, maybe.

About the Author

Steve Brezenoff lives in St. Paul, Minnesota with his wife, Beth, and their small, brave dog, Harry. Besides writing books, he enjoys playing video games, riding his bicycle, and helping high school students to improve their own writing skills. Steve's ideas almost always come to him in dreams, so he does his best writing in his pajamas.

About the Illustrator

Phillip Hilliker lives most of his life in the strange and creepy realm in his head. Becoming an illustrator was pretty much the only career path that would allow him to stay there. Phil graduated from the College for Creative Studies and has spent the majority of the past few years illustrating various role-playing-game books. He lives in Arizona with his awesome scientist of a wife and their imaginary pet bunny, Balthazar.

Glossary

brave (BRAVE)—if you are brave, you show courage and are willing to do difficult things

headquarters (HED-quor-turz)—the place from which an organization or group is run

initiation (i-nish-ee-AY-shuhn)—the ceremony or test that brings someone into a group

mansion (MAN-shuhn)—a very large and grand house

option (OP-shuhn)—a choice

paramedics (pa-ruh-MED-iks)—people who respond to emergency medical situations

poison (POI-zuhn)—if you poison someone, you give them a substance that can harm them

shelter (SHEL-tur)—a place where a homeless person can stay

skeleton key (SKEL-uh-ton KEE)—a key that can open every room in a house

suspects (SUH-spekts)—people thought to be responsible for a crime

Discussion Questions

1. Did Kayla do the right thing when she accepted the dare to stay overnight in the old mansion? Why or why not?

2. Do you think the people in this book are brave? Talk about what the word brave means. Can you think of other examples of brave people?

3. Would you want to be a member of the Braves? Why or why not?

Writing Prompts

1. Have you ever been in a club? Write about it. If you haven't been in a club, make one up. What would your club do?

2. During the summer, the kids in this book spend time together. What do you like to do during the summer? Who do you like to hang out with?

3. At the end of this book, Gutter says that the Braves had many more adventures. Make up an adventure that you think the Braves had. Write about it!

MORE ABOUT

When most people think about mushrooms, they picture a small, spongy, white plant with a little cap. Those are called white button mushrooms, and are often served on salads. But that's only one kind of mushrooms. In fact, more than 14,000 different mushrooms have been identified!

Mushrooms are a form of fungus. A fungus is a type of plant that has no leaves or any green growing parts.

While some mushrooms are used for eating, others are used to make medicines and drugs. Still others are poisonous. Some dangerous mushrooms can cause hallucinations or fevers. Others can even cause death.

MUSHROOMS

People have been using mushrooms for thousands of years. And not just for food. Some mushrooms have been used to dye fabrics. Some were used as fire starters — in fact, one mummy found in Italy, who had died about 5,000 years ago, was found carrying dried mushrooms that he would have used to start fires.

Because there are so many varieties of mushrooms in the world, you should never eat a mushroom that you find outdoors. In fact, unless you are a skilled mushroom expert, you have no way of knowing what type of mushroom you've found. Some deadly mushrooms look just like safe ones. It's smarter (and safer) to try the different varieties of mushrooms you can find in the produce section at your grocery store.

Internet Sites

Do you want to know more about subjects
related to this book? Or are you interested in
learning about other topics? Then check out
FactHound, a fun, easy way to find Internet sites.

Our investigative staff has already sniffed out
great sites for you!

Here's how to use FactHound:

1. Visit *www.facthound.com*

2. Select your grade level.

3. To learn more about subjects related
   to this book, type in the book's ISBN number:
   9781434207982.

4. Click the **Fetch It** button.

FactHound will fetch the best Internet sites for
you!